A Gift to Aafji

A Pella Christmas Story

ALSO BY MARCUS BACH

Who Stole My Utopia?

I, Monty

Whispers from Wildlife

The World of Serendipity

The Unity Way of Life

Because of Christmas

Spiritual Breakthroughs for Our Time

The Power of Total Living

The Power of Perfect Liberty

The Power of Perception

The Will to Believe

Questions on the Quest

God and the Soviets

Inside Voodoo

Major Religions of the World

The Challenge of Change

Strange Altars

A Gift to Aafji

A Pella Christmas Story

MARCUS BACH

Illustrations by Joseph and Dawnelle Engesser

A GIFT to AAFJI: A Pella Christmas Story

Library of Congress No. 92-064495
ISBN 0-9624320-3-2

First Edition, First Printing
Printed in the United States of America

Published by SUNBURST PUBLISHING
Suite 224 · 520 S. Pierce
Mason City, Iowa 50401

The book is available at special discounts on bulk purchases for sales promotions, premiums, fundraising or educational use. For details, contact the Special Sales Department, Sunburst Publishing, 520 S. Pierce, Suite 224, Mason City, Iowa 50401.

To the people
of Pella,
pioneers in the spirit
and culture
of the
American tradition.

Briefly...

With the exception of Aafji, all persons and situations in *A Gift to Aafji* are entirely fictional. Although Aafji is modeled on a prominent 19th century Pella citizen, Miss Siebertje Viersen, the times, situations and other individuals in *A Gift to Aafji* are gifts to us from the author's delightful imagination.

--The Publisher

1.

Just before the Christmas season in 1933 when there were twelve million jobless in the U.S.A. and the credit crunch and bankruptcies bedeviled even the thrifty Dutch of Pella, Iowa, the owner of Tulip Town's embroidery shop announced that she was quitting business.

Miss Aafji de Haan let it be known through the pages of the Pella Weekly Gazette that all bills due her became payable immediately, and she added this ultimatum:

"All persons who do not settle up within ten days, to them I will come and take out the amount of said bill in board and lodging until same is satisfied."

The drying up of world trade and the developing Federal Works projects were far-off events. The possibility of Aafji invading your home with Christmas in the offing was something personal and immediate. The announcement prompted a rash of penny auctions and considerable activity in borrowing, for Aafji had done an immense business in the past twenty years --- a great deal on credit.

Several people managed to pay up and certainly everyone tried. One woman sold her chickens. Another got a pawnshop loan on her wedding ring in nearby Des Moines. An otherwise good member of the Dutch Reformed Church admitted she transferred her tithing money from the Lord to Aafji rather than have the embroiderer invade her premises.

Aafji

Aafji, forty-seven, gaunt and strong, just sat sewing. She sewed even though she was closing up shop. Or else she stood behind her plank counter, arms folded across her flat, mannish bosom, her cold eyes shaming the devil. Why she had trusted people so long and dunned them so little was Aafji's business. Some said it was because she had been jilted in love before she moved to Pella from Holland, Michigan. She was out to show the Pella people she could make it on her own.

The shears of time snipped off the days without any regard for the folks who dreaded Aafji's deadline. In homes where there were children, the question was, "Does Aafji have to come to our house?" People watched her apprehensively while her old-fashioned shoes --- made straight so they could be worn on either foot --- came down like mallets on the sidewalks of the town.

At the end of the tenth day of Aafji's threat Pella Square was deserted. It was six o'clock. The dimly lighted stores had a forsaken look even with their Christmas decorations. No one was on the streets.

2.

Heer Ypi van Gorp sat stubbornly in his straight-backed rocking chair with his house at his back.

Ypi, who had come all the way from the old country to call Pella his kingdom, gripped his long Dutch pipe determinedly. Ypi was forty-eight, but he would not have been offended if anyone had told him he was an old man. He had been old at thirty-five when he came from Rotterdam to Pella to start the brick kiln.

Ypi loved nothing better than his liberties. He owed Aafji a bill, but he would have no cash until the first of

Sitting Guard

the year. He had never borrowed money, and he did not intend to start now. Anyway, he contended that his bill was nineteen dollars and eighteen cents, and Aafji said it was twenty eighty-one.

Ypi's home, next to Banker Scholte's, was one of the largest in town. It had twelve rooms and Ypi occupied them all. For going on eight years he had had nothing but unfortunate experiences trying to share the rooms with a wife, Engeltji, and they were always in each other's way. She left him before Christmas a year ago, and as far as he was concerned it was good riddance.

Thoughts of the ex-Mrs. van Gorp flitted through Ypi's mind as he sucked at his pipe on this early December evening. Engeltji, to be sure, had caused him a good deal of trouble and, what was worse, expense. The bill to Aafji was really Engeltji's. She had wanted to put curtains on the windows. Curtains would have kept out the light and upped the light bills. Engeltji could not understand that. Engeltji wanted expensive hats and a beaver muff to keep up with Banker Scholte's wife.

A GIFT TO AAFJI

Ypi sat with both feet firmly on the thick oak boards of his porch. He was a short, round man with a square red face in which every feature was a stern, engraved line. His shock of hair, prematurely white, was kept covered by a black hat from beneath which tufts of sideburns crept down his cheeks. He wore a black silk vest and a frock coat. He always carried a cane, partly for companionship, but also because of a discernible limp following an accident at the kiln. These were acquisitions dating from the post-Engeltji period. Pella said that Ypi dressed like a retired gentleman ever since the day he and Engeltji separated and she went to live with an aunt in Des Moines. Engeltji had always shamed him because he usually went the livelong day in work clothes, bearing the dust and stain of the kiln.

3.

Suddenly, on this particular evening, Pella Square held its breath and, for a moment, the town's silence crystallized. Aafji had opened the door of her shop and was coming out. She was armed with a carpet bag and an umbrella. She closed the door with a solid bang and fastened the lock. Every sound she made echoed in the brittle, chilly December dusk. Tonight she seemed taller and sterner than ever. The corners of her mouth were pulled down. Her purple scarf, worn snugly over her combed-back hair, had a yellow Christmas star embroidered meticulously to fit the exact center of her forehead. She swept her eyes across the square and turned to measure her field of conquest.

In his sturdy chair, Ypi felt every rivet in his rotund frame tighten. He took his pipe from between his teeth and clamped his jaws. He saw Aafji turn in his direction and thought he heard her sniff the air. He noticed figures peering from the darkening windows of the stores and saw a group of youngsters draw out of her way as she haughtily strode by, straight as a ramrod, her pleated skirt dusting the sidewalk.

Aafji came across Pella Square straight as an arrow. Her face was aimed at Ypi, but her eyes over-shot his in that disturbing way she had. She seemed rather to be headed right over him and on into the house. The nearer she came the more Ypi drew back in his chair, but there was a limit to how far he could go. By the time Aafji's loud, hammered strides brought her to the porch, Ypi's chin was pulled turtle-like into the neck of his cravat. The store doors began to open slowly. The youngsters stood by watching.

Stern Beginning

It was not want of courage that momentarily defeated Ypi, it was sheer abjection. The thought that he was first on Aafji's list substantiated a fear he had harbored all along. Ypi had always been superstitious, and this added a few more poisonous drops.

"Heer van Gorp," announced Aafji, "I am here!"

Ypi's neck came out of his cravat slowly, and he took her measure from head to foot. Then he laid his pipe aside and brought both hands down on the arms of his chair.

"And here I am!" he said defiantly. "You don't play this crazy game on me!"

"Crazy it may be," said Aafji, "but it at least gets me what's mine. Twenty dollars and eighty-one cents is, as I figure, nine days and a half!"

"Nine days and a half!" roared Ypi. "Nine and a half minutes will be the limit under my roof!"

He hobbled his chair until it was exactly in front of the door.

"Hih!" was all that Aafji said and, with a tilt of her head, she walked smack around the chair and straight into the house.

"Hey!" shouted Ypi, jumping to his feet with the aid of his cane. "You come out of there!"

He followed her in, bolstered by his verbal barrage about getting the sheriff and about there having been no woman in those rooms for going on two years.

"It looks like it!" was Aafji's retort. Then she said stiffly, "Where is my room?"

"Woman," said Ypi, "don't be a damn fool! You aren't staying here, and I won't have you stay. You can say I owe you a bill, and if you make it the correct amount I will pay it when I can."

"When you can!" exclaimed Aafji. "It's been two years standing. A year before your wife ran out on you."

"Legally it was her bill, not mine," he retorted. "I have no need for embroidery."

"It is said you never gave her any money for anything," was Aafji's retort.

Ypi brought his cane down with a bang on the floor. "To scandal and gossip you are not going to set me up or this will be something for the law!"

Aafji did not deign to reply. Scandal and gossip were words beyond her ken. She knew of nothing she had ever done that was not in keeping with sound ethics. Nothing else mattered. And to answer Ypi van Gorp would have been a waste of words out of all keeping with her views of economy. She spied a bedroom, made her way to it, went in, and shut the door.

4.

Had it not been evening, Ypi would certainly have had reason to think that the sudden shadow which fell over the house was a wraith raised by Aafji's presence, for when the bedroom door slammed shut, a perceptible semi-darkness enveloped the rooms.

Ypi told himself that this always happened on December nights, but it was scary.

For two cents he would go over to Banker Scholte's, borrow some money, pay the bill and let it go at that, but then the town talk would see how clever Aafji was and of how once in his life Heer van Gorp had met his equal. It was a choice of two evils and, in keeping with Ypi's tradition, he always chose the one that saved him money and pride.

He hobbled around in the room clasping and unclasping his hands. Then Aafji suddenly appeared.

"When do we eat?" she asked bluntly.

"Woman!" stormed Ypi. "Stop this foolishness! Take your things and get out before I put you out!"

"Hih!" said Aafji, and she walked past him in the direction of the kitchen.

Ypi said, "God damnit!" and the blood rushed to his face.

The room grew darker. He glared at the windows, half expecting to see a specter of Engeltji pulling down curtains of gloom. He assured himself it was simply the way of the Advent season. Pella Square reflected the full, dark canopy of the sky. It was getting colder. Ypi decided to go to Banker Scholte and ask his advice. The banker did not like to be bothered after hours, but, figured Ypi, there was no other way.

He went to the shelf to get his hat, discovered when he got there that the hat was on his head, had been on his head all the time. He seized his walking stick from the back of the chair and headed toward the door. In the kitchen Aafji was rattling dishes. The smell of wood-smoke began to fill the rooms. Ypi veered around and went out to where Aafji was stuffing more fuel into the stove.

"You've got the draft shut!" he shouted, going to the stove and making an adjustment. "Is this a smoke house?"

"I will fix myself thirty-five cents worth for supper," said Aafji, without pausing in her work. "That is what I figure for the evening meal on the nine-and-a-half-day basis and will fix myself some mush and bake myself an apple!"

"You can fix yourself arsenic!" fumed Ypi. "For two cents I would throw you out with my own hands."

"Cornmeal mush and molasses is what I'll fix for myself," she said, pulling open a cupboard door and bringing out the cornmeal and salt as if she knew exactly where they had been stored.

"Make yourself the cornmeal mush," he said disdainfully, "but don't think I don't know that you saw the pail of sorghum on the front porch when you came in. That was just given me by Heer Van der Waals on whom they foreclosed his mill."

"I'll help myself to just a quarter cup of it," Aafji decided, reaching for a glass.

"Oh, no, you don't," Ypi responded. "I'll bring it in

so that nothing will be spilled. Yes, you can have a quarter cup, but the rest goes into jars and stored away for winter use."

With this he strode out with as much authority as he could muster and soon returned with the gallon pail.

"You see," Aafji's taunting voice reported, "you spilled some of it yourself. It is still dripping all over the floor."

"Mind yourself!" warned Ypi, as he took a wash cloth and went back to clean up whatever had happened when he had angrily seized the sorghum pail from the porch. Aafji spied the quart-sized fruit jars he had on the kitchen counter ready to receive the dark, rich fruit of the sorghum mill. She was just pouring in the first syrupy stream when there was the sound of clawing and mumbling on the porch. It was something of a commotion, but her resolute hands poured the sorghum into the jars without spilling a drop.

Then an agonizing groan floated in to her through the deepening shadows. She started out. Ypi lay on the porch flat on his back, one leg sticking through the rungs of the chair.

"Don't touch me!" he warned.

Aafji extricated his leg, while he gritted his teeth. Then she started back to the door, turning to ask, "Can you get up?"

"Damn you, woman!" said Ypi.

"Are you hurt? If you aren't hurt, why don't you get up?

"Put the chair over here for me to hold on to and I'll make it good enough," he told her.

She maneuvered the chair over to him and, after some searching, located his cane. Also his hat. She handed them to him, and he accepted them. but try as he might,

Ypi Falls

he could not get to his feet. He struggled and groaned and sought to lift himself, but it was no use. The pain grew worse. Soon he fell back from sheer exhaustion, moaning and wiping the perspiration from his face.

Throughout this demonstration, Aafji stood with her arms folded, resolute and expressionless. When Ypi finally gave up, she bent her tall, lanky body down, put her arm around his shoulders, compelled him to put his arm around her neck, and raised him up. She dragged him into the house, his plump form dangling, his feet barely scraping the floor.

"Where's your room?" she asked.

"Let me down anywhere," he panted.

"You maybe broke your hip. You are sweating and you could take cold."

Ypi told her his room was upstairs.

"Then use mine," said Aafji.

"*Mine!*" reverberated Ypi. "Woman, if you had never come, this would never have happened!"

"Things happen the way they're supposed to happen," said Aafji as she hauled him to her room, and made him stretch out as best he could on the bed. Pain and fury notwithstanding, he heard her words with alarm. They were the echo of Engeltji's philosophy which he too had struggled with for years. Things, somehow, usually happened the way they always happened -- to him.

"Was anybody to blame the time you broke your leg at the kiln?" asked Aafji, getting him on the bed. "Nobody. It was supposed to be. It was supposed to be that your wife Engeltji was here to take care of you at that time."

"It is bad enough to have you around," said Ypi. "Don't preach church doctrine to me."

"Do you want me to turn a light on?" she asked.

"If I want one, *I* will."

She took her carpet bag and umbrella and went from the room, stomping on upstairs to find a room of her own.

5.

Ypi was often to look back on this moment as one of the gloomiest of his life. Never in his nearly fifty years had the bottom dropped out of things so completely. He had been dumped as unceremoniously on the bed as a gunnysack of broken bricks from his now bankrupt kiln. The room was dark and cold and the sullen hand of doom had closed the door.

Worst of all was the fact that this particular bedroom was haunted by the memory of Engeltji. For a number of weeks during their estrangement she had made this her domicile. He seemed to see her everywhere now, in the ghastly gloom of the oval walnut mirror, at the window where the gray twilight had dissolved to black and shadows. He felt her sitting at his side, quietly stroking his hand as she had done following his accident at the kiln. That time Engeltji had always brought him his favorite dessert: baked apples.

Now he heard footsteps come down from upstairs. Then the front door was opened and banged shut. In the haunting evening quiet, Ypi heard Aafji leave the house. He heard her solid, hard stomps on the porch, then down the steps, and heard them fade and die away.

A wave of relief and peace came over him. He had insulted her off the place, and that was exactly what she deserved. He had his freedom. To have kept this woman under his roof one single night would have made him the laughing stock of the town. He rubbed his chin, but a tendency to smile was obliterated when he tried to get up. He felt he was badly hurt. His hip was numb, and his right leg ached. He could scarcely stir.

Furthermore, he was hungry.

The thought of Aafji, or any woman, leaving a man helpless and in pain was harassing. Glad as he was to think she was gone, it nettled him when he contemplated the full measure of female ingratitude. Not even mush had she offered him, let alone a baked apple. He tried laboriously to extricate himself from his coat and remove his shoes, but finally gave up.

Long minutes later the klomp-klomp of Aafji de Haan sounded unmistakably back on the porch. Night was settling down, and the house of Ypi van Gorp was in darkness. But Aafji turned on lights all over the place, in the front room, in the kitchen and in the bedroom as she came in.

"He is in the country," she announced.

"Who?"

"Doctor van Zee. His wife told me what to do with

you and what to feed you till he comes."

"How in thunder does she know what to do with me when she doesn't know what's wrong?"

"I gave her symptoms. How you were able to get onto the bed without too much pain and all. She said it was likely nothing more than an aggravation."

"An aggravation!" Ypi exploded. Then, with concern, "What's more, I'm cold. Did you tell her that? I'm cold!"

"She said we should get you warm," said Aafji, rolling up her sleeves. "You should undress and I should get you under the covers. She sent along a hot water bottle. I'll get everything ready while you undress."

"Undress?" Ypi yelled. "How should I get out of my pants, woman, in the shape I'm in?"

"Try it," said Aafji over her shoulder on her way out.

"I can help when I applicate you with the hot water bottle."

"Devil!" groaned Ypi. "No woman is going to take off my pants and applicate me!"

He tried to get out of his clothes, but it was no use. He was cold and one thing Ypi always feared was a chill. Somehow, he had to get under the covers.

Aafji returned as he was working his way out of his coat. She made it look easy as she assisted him.

"The water is just about hot," she said reassuringly, then asked, "Where is it?"

"Where is what?" asked Ypi.

"The sore spot," said Aafji. "The place where I should apply the water bottle."

He could only glower at her. Her presence was as

painful as the injury. He saw her there, standing at the foot of the bed, her scarf with the star making her look like a medicine man. All she needed were horns.

"The water will get cold," she informed him politely, "if we don't know where to applicate it."

"Let it freeze if it's a mind to!" he retorted.

She left the room only to return in a miraculously short time with the hot water bottle and a huge towel in her arms. With no fooling around she put these things aside and began pulling the covers out from under him. Deaf to his protestations, she manipulated him so that he was lying on the sheet. She was now at the foot of the bed with her hands clinched to the cuffs of his trousers. Then she remembered to remove his shoes.

"Woman!" shouted Ypi, "have you gone mad?"

"Loosen the pants," said Aafji, "and I'll pull." She jerked warningly with her sturdy fingers on the cuffs.

Standing Her Ground

Ypi lay at bay. He had to confess he could not move. Sharp pains criss-crossed through his hip. He longed for the water bottle with the towel around it. He moaned and thought of Engeltji and, from sheer exhaustion, he permitted Aafji to have her way.

Then she was telling him to, "Say when!" by which she meant when he had loosened his belt and unbuttoned the flap which Ypi did, while stammering through gritted teeth, "P-Pull!"

Aafji responded like a draft horse, relieving him of his trousers with her usual impersonal, business-like precision. Ypi was far from being dishabille, for he always wore a number of under garments and practically sewed himself up for the winter, but he shouted to Aafji to turn off the light and hand him the hot water bottle.

She said not a word. She left the light burning, wrapped the towel "application" and applied it just below the hip where Ypi held his hand where it hurt, while his other hand covered an "obscenity" as best he could.

Embarrassing Application

Aafji said, "By the time it cools off, I will have you some more warm."

Tucking the blankets over him gently, she left him on his own. Yet, with the precision of a mill wheel and just as impersonally she kept coming around to inquire about his aggravations. He began to actually look forward to her visitations and on the fifth of them she suddenly appeared at his bedside with a baked apple.

"What's this?" Ypi wanted to know.

"The doctor's wife's orders," Aafji explained. "You're supposed to eat."

The more Ypi saw of her giant and graceless figure and her expressionlessly carved face, the more he groaned in his spirit, groans of incongruity about the way things happened to him, groans of self-pity seasoned with a touch of wonder. And as he munched on the apple, he heard himself say with a touch of gentleness, "Engeltji always put brown sugar on them."

"I couldn't find any brown sugar," said Aafji, already on her way out. "I'd have put some on, too, if I could have found it."

"You seem to find everything else," he retaliated. "But before you spend a night in this house, you're going to be paid off and you can go." And he lay back, chewing thoughtfully on the warm and juicy apple, savoring it with many a fleeting thought.

Ever since his boyhood when he picked apples with his father in Rotterdam, ever since his mother baked them for him, ever since Engeltji, baked apples had implanted a life-long craving. He missed the brown sugary taste and should have told Aafji where the ingredient was stored. His stubbornness had defeated his own purpose, but, savoring her serving, it dawned on him that she had thoughtfully flavored his apple with sorghum, reserved usually just for mush. There was something resourceful about Aafji, when he got to thinking about it.

6.

When the doctor finally put in his appearance, Ypi had a head full of ideas.

"Let me give her the nineteen dollars and eighteen cents," he told Doctor van Zee, "and we'll get her packing out of here tonight."

"Now, let's see," mused the doctor, "do we want her to go?"

"*Want her to go?*"

"You have a badly bruised thigh, Heer van Gorp."

"*That* I can help with applications," said Ypi. "Her I can't!"

"Who is to bring you the applications if you get her to go?"

"I can get people who don't make me feel worse every time they come in the room."

Doctor van Zee, who was sixty-five and thoughtful of speech, rubbed the side of his nose. With his way of sensing out details, he observed that the "application" had been properly applied and also that a dish with a bit of apple core had been licked ravishingly clean with only a trace of sorghum remaining on the spoon.

"Oh," he agreed resourcefully, "if you don't mind about expense, I can get you a nurse all right. That's what you need. But Aafji de Haan is working for nothing, as I understand, and doing right well. You will save both the embroidery bill and the cost of a nurse if you keep her. That means something these days with the depression and all. It is not like the days when you were profitably baking loaves of bricks in the famous van Gorp kiln."

The words gave Ypi solemn pause. His personal account, which was desperately low, testified to his dwindling business judgment. The dire prospects of a sojourn with Aafji did hold some justification.

"I have always been a fair man, Doctor van Zee," Ypi argued. "What's more I must say she is the kind of a woman you don't have to treat different than you feel like treating her. A barn door would get you just as much attention. As for nursing me, she takes things too much in her own hands like she did with getting me out of my pants and here in bed."

"But she did accomplish her purpose," mused Doctor van Zee. "Remember the saying we always had in Rotterdam --- 'A bee without a sting makes no honey?'

Better it had been to have honey on your baked apple than sorghum."

Ypi looked at him long and almost tenderly. "Best of all," he said quietly, "would have been brown sugar."

7.

Three days dragged on during the course of these events, but neither Aafji nor Ypi had any intention of getting their relationship on a basis other than that which the first night had established.

Aafji spent most of her day time with her needlework and attending to her shop, and Ypi drove himself to make premature progress with a pair of crutches that he had saved from the time of the kiln accident. Aafji came faithfully to prepare his meals which were palatable and never extravagant. Neighbors sometimes brought pastries. But no matter what happened Ypi never squeezed a smile out of Aafji, and she rarely wrung a kind word out of him.

On the night of the third day, when Aafji came in with an armful of wood for the living room stove, she found an *aanspreker* with Ypi. This man was Pella's lawyer, Hendrik Heemstra, and a much respected, busy person. He would never have been found at Ypi van Gorp's home or away from his office had it not been that this evening he was cast in the role of *aanspreker*. An old man, a friend of Heer Heemstra, had died early that morning and in keeping with a Dutch custom, someone had to go from door to door and announce the death to every household in a solemn and dignified manner. This was Hendrik Heemstra's mission.

Dressed in a dark business suit, a wide band of black crepe on his left arm, white gloves, a silken top hat, he had been going slowly from house to house with his sad refrain. He was not supposed to enter, only knock, and convey his message at the open door. In fact, it was considered a very bad omen to have an *aanspreker* enter

The Aanspreker

one's home. At van Gorp's, however, his knock had been greeted by Ypi's loud cry of, "Come in!" since Aafji was out at the woodpile at the time. Out of deference to Ypi's injury, Heer Heemstra had entered. Ypi, seeing it was an *aanspreker*, was too shaken for words. It was Aafji, pausing long enough with the wood, who inquired about the death and then went on with her duties.

"Lawyer Heemstra," said Ypi, seated in a chair and clasping his crutches before him in both hands, "you can see what trouble has already fallen upon me without an *aanspreker's* visit. But," he continued gropingly, "maybe it is all for the good for a change. Maybe you, being a lawyer, can tell me how to get this embroiderer out of my house."

"Sorry, Heer van Gorp," said Heer Heemstra, "this is not my mission. Furthermore, if you ordered her off the premises, she might put in a bill for taking care of you these past days."

"Taking care of me!" Ypi exclaimed. "Who asked her to come? Not I, for sure!"

"It was all quite legal, her coming here," lawyer Heemstra took time to say. "She put the warning of her debt collecting into the public press. And her loyalty to you in your time of need also stands her in good stead. There is talk in the town how fortunate you are to have her. To turn her out now could be both expensive and technical from the point of law. Perhaps a court trial and all."

"A court trial?" Ypi echoed. "Oh, by God, now!"

The *aanspreker* prepared to leave, but, being a gentle person, he said, "Aafji de Haan was by no means obligated to play nursemaid to you. There is the matter of what the law calls 'care claim.'"

A strange, nostalgic yearning suddenly came over Ypi as thoughts of the law closed in. Just now he felt alone, miserably alone, in a world he had not made. There was a needed strength he did not have. There was a method of adjustment to situations that was not in him. Miserable indeed was the world, and miserable was the way of a woman like Aafji de Haan. And yet .....

In a moment he found himself pouring out his heart to the *aanspreker.* Aafji, Ypi surmised in deep confession, would outlive him. Long after he was gone, Pella would hear the firm stomp of her feet on its walkways. Life, he agonized, is for the strong. He had always borne the weight of the world, but never as much as now. Even the uncertainty of America's future was linked to his own incapacitated state and bore down upon him like Job's burdens of guilt. How was it that out of all her customers, Aafji had chosen to come first to him? How was it that he had to slip and fall because of molasses?

"When I pass on," Ypi soliloquized, "who will be my *aanspreker.* And how you say the town is siding up with Aafji de Haan." He shook his head. "Like Job," he heard himself say, "the things I was afraid would happen have happened."

This plunged him into deeper despair. To think that he would have mentioned Job, not having had much truck with religion along the way. To think of Job at Christmas time...instead of remembering what happened in Bethlehem...

The *aanspreker* had been a generous listener, but now he was on his feet and, pressing Ypi's hand reassuringly, he apologized for having entered, then walked solemnly from the room.

8.

Moments passed. A moon rose from behind the low and silent buildings on the Square, while Aafji came in and fluffed up an extra pillow, adjusting it behind his head to make sitting up less strenuous.

"I am fixing mush and baked apples," she said.

"I'm not hungry," Ypi murmured.

"You must eat," she cautioned, "or you'll get sick."

"All right," he allowed, "then I get sick."

Aafji took his hand gently and he was too bewildered to resist. Instead, he looked at her in awe as she reached into the pocket of her apron and pulled out a brightly multi-colored piece of cloth. She unfolded it gracefully and displayed it for his approval.

"You said you often felt cold," she confided, "and I thought you might have a sore throat on top of everything. In my things at the store I found this cravat I once embroidered. Here, I will put it on you. It is woolen, like a warm and gentle compress."

She tucked it around his neck with expert precision and the reason he did not resist was because he was in silent shock. The episode came with a suddenness and an authority that thoroughly undid any protest. Furthermore he felt an instant warmth coursing through his body as if she had wrapped him in hot water bottles. He could feel his heart beating and it was as if the flannel feeling of the neckpiece was clearing his throat.

Speechless, he watched her seat herself at the round bedside table and lose herself in a period of needlework. She sat there, enviously industrious, a testimony to the deepest of Dutch commitments: *make the most of time while it is still yours.*

She sat there, lips compressed into thin lines, shoulders erect. Irresolutely, Ypi studied her. If, as some people seemed to believe, she was gaining the town's respect, what was he to say? And where did this leave him, with nothing but time on his hands?

She returned to the kitchen. Ypi heard the oven door open with its customary yawnish squeak. Engeltji had often ordered him to fix it. Aafji would probably applicate some lard on it and that was all it needed.

Engeltji Arrives

9.

In the darkening out-of-doors several lanterns moved through the deepening dusk, lanterns and candle bearers.

Out of the distance came the sound of caroling ever so faint. So faint it was rudely interrupted by the rattling sound of a car stopping abruptly in front of Ypi's home. After a brief pause, the vehicle took off as noisily as it had come. Soon the sound of footsteps on the front porch were climaxed by a resounding knock on the door. Aafji came quickly from the kitchen.

"See who it is," Ypi ordered. "If it is more bad news, let's have it over with."

Aafji went to the door. A woman's voice, soft and chastened, drifted into the room. It inquired about Heer van Gorp and in another moment the slender, attractive form of Engeltji appeared in the doorway. She had never looked lovelier. An expensive fur hat was pressed down snugly on her blonde hair, her dress was bright beneath a soft wrap-around coat, and her hands were tucked inside a comfortable beaver muff.

"Ypi!" she greeted, hurrying to his side. "Were you hurt bad when you slipped and fell?"

He tried to answer, but his lips trembled and his eyes traveled uneasily to Aafji pausing just inside the room.

"You look good, Ypi!" Engeltji extolled, removing her coat and tossing it with her muff on a chair. "You look nice! And what a pretty cravat! I never remember you ever wearing a neck scarf! How do you feel? Can you walk?"

"I take steps," he managed to say, but at that he stopped, for she had taken his hand and was pressing it warmly. Her blue eyes swept his, and she looked at him long and lovingly as if sincerely full of joy.

Ypi chewed his lips as if eating words he wanted desperately to articulate. He could sense a tenderness in Engeltji's voice. She looked different. She was a new person.

Again he cast a nervous eye at Aafji, measuring her with a glance while she remained lost in a night of sudden loneliness. Just then he felt a strange remorse and pity for her. She was no longer self-sufficient, she was instead quite desolate. There was nothing worse than to have no one at all in the world, and that was how she suddenly appeared to him.

Engeltji was telling him how word had reached her about his accident. She told him of the ride on the bus and of how she had sat next to a woman who was coming to Pella for a funeral. And she told him that she got to thinking about life and how brief it was, and how wonderful it was to see him again. She had come just on impulse --- worried and wondering how she would be received. She spoke as though they were alone in the big house, and during her talking Aafji faded from view, going silently to the kitchen. Ypi quietly stroked Engeltji's hands.

"It is really good to see you," he confessed. "Things have been going mighty bad. And as for expense, it costs just as much as when you were here. Even more."

Engeltji laughed low and pleased. Ypi felt a certain strength creeping into his heart. A load was being taken from him. The room seemed to have grown brighter. The cravat gave him a certain confidence.

"You -- take off your things, Engeltji," he said. "You stay."

Her eyes grew soft.

"Your voice has a different tone, Ypi," she said quietly "and the way you look -- dressed up -- I never imagined."

The sombre form of Aafji returned to the room. She was carrying a tray on which cornbread and two baked apples announced themselves with their own aroma. Engeltji saw, sensed, and smelled them all at once and the sensations brought her to Aafji's side.

"I'll take the tray, Miss de Haan," she said, suiting action to her words. "Baked apples, Ypi!'

The most wonderful thing of all, thought Ypi, was the fact that Engeltji asked no questions. She betrayed no suspicion. She showed no surprise. She took everything for granted, as though she had been away only a few days and now had pleasantly returned.

"You can go now," Engletji told Aafji, as she set the

tray on the table. "I will take things over."

"Mrs. van Gorp," Aafji explained, "I am here only on the matter of collecting a bill. Figured on a day-by-day basis, there is nine dollars and fifty cents still remaining."

"That we can settle," said Engeltji, and her hands dove into her muff from which she extracted a beaded purse and began to count out ten one dollar bills.

"I learned of the situation the moment I came to town," Engeltji admitted sincerely, pressing the bills into Aafji's hands. "Keep the change, Miss de Haan, and thank you for all the good care you took of Mijnheer van Gorp."

"Now, Engeltji!" Ypi began protestingly, but as he saw the two women face-to-face as if in a common bond of understanding, his eyes grew wide. Between "the woman" and Engeltji there passed a glance that was vocal. For the first time, someone was offering her more than what she considered her rightul dues. This robbed

Face-to-Face

her of a desire to claim more. For an instant, her stout, angular form sagged. Then she stiffened with pride and drew herself tall. She had never done anything by halves and it was not her intention to do so now.

"Things," she said firmly, "are the way they ought to be. I am woman enough to know that."

The voice was Aafji's but for a moment a mask dropped from her face. Tenderness and resignation, mingled with a deep longing, reflected in her eyes. She laid the money determinedly on the table and went quickly from the room, leaving Engeltji to protest.

10.

When Aafji returned she was dressed to go out, and she carried her carpet bag and her umbrella in steady hands.

Most of all, and what held Engeltji enthralled beyond words, was the scarf Aafji was wearing, the scarf with the Star of Christmas magnificently embellished with unmistakable skill. Engeltji was tempted to comment on it, for she could hardly take her eyes away from the star's fascination. In the best stores in Des Moines she had never seen anything like it. What a sale such a headcovering would have prompted had Aafji only been progressive and in keeping with the times! Someday, Engeltji vowed within herself, she would have to talk business with Aafji de Haan, especially if the depression ever ended. For now, she tried again to give Aafji the money.

"Please take it," she urged. "I was blessed with quite a family inheritance since my days here in Pella."

"Yes, yes," Ypi agreed, his face glowing in remembrance of what once had been an intolerable shock, the inheritance coming hard on the heels of their separation and he not having shared in any of it.

That was the breaking point as far as Aafji was concerned. To think that Ypi had held the matter of the inheritance in mind was, to her, unthinkable. Resolutely she reached for the ten one dollar bills.

"Things are the way they ought to be," she repeated with finality and tucked the money into her carpet bag.

Then she laid two quarters on the table. "There is your change, and may Heer van Gorp reimburse you since the bill was under his name in the first place."

Ypi's momentary show of embarrassment was Aafji's greatest reward.

"There is mush ready to fry in the kitchen," Aafji informed Engeltji. "Enough for the two of you. And may you have a good night."

As she turned determinedly to take her leave, she was stopped dead in her tracks by four short, sharp resounding rings of the kitchen telephone.

This was the first time during her self-imposed stay at the van Gorp domicile that the phone had ever rung Ypi's number: four short blasts. It was a party line, but never once had it been heard ringing for Ypi or, possibly, for Aafji de Haan. Without thinking, Aafji dropped her belongings and was about to rush to answer when Engeltji beat her to the call. Nonetheless, Aafji could not pull herself away. She remained waiting and exchanging questions with Ypi about who could possibly be at the other end of the line. Ypi showed great concern and when Engeltji returned, sweeping past Aafji and coming directly to him, he could only feel trouble ahead.

It didn't help when Engeltji announced excitedly, "It was the mayor, Mayor Wybenga! He called to warn you, Ypi, that he is on his way over here and wanted you to be sure and have the porch light burning!"

Ypi had come to his feet, leaning heavily on his crutches. "Mayor Wybenga! What does he want?"

"He didn't say," said Engeltji. "He didn't even ask who was answering the phone. He was in a great hurry."

"It's the law!" Ypi concluded. "It sounds like something to do with a care claim! What next? How much more can befall a man?"

"I'll be going," said Aafji reaching for her umbrella and carpet bag.

"You stay!" Ypi commanded. "Turn on the porch light. The mayor is not one to waste any time."

"Maybe he is coming because he heard I came to town," Engeltji figured. "He must remember me from the Christmas party four years ago. Remember, Ypi, when the kiln was the talk of the town and things were going so well with us?"

Ypi didn't know whether to laugh or cry, whether to send Engeltji packing or thank her for coming to his side as she now did consolingly. It all happened so fast and now the phone was ringing again, but this time it wasn't four short rings. It was three short and one long and, obviously, for someone else. Still it was a shocker and hardly had Aafji turned on the porch light and seized a broom to sweep the steps and tidy things up outside than here came the mayor in his private Ford roadster with its brass polished headlights gleaming.

11.

There was Aafji on the porch with the broom, there were Ypi and Engeltji just appearing in the open doorway, braving the cold, when the rotund and agile Mayor Wybenga came bounding up the steps.

"*Vroolijke Kerstmis!*" he greeted, sweeping his hat from his balding head in exaggerated style.

"It may be too early for a 'Merry Christmas,'" he greeted graciously. "It may be too early, but something has happened for which Des Moines newsmen are waiting in my office to cover. We have no time to lose."

"Ah, Aafji de Hann!" he announced, coming to her and taking her hands in his, "you must make a quick decision! Reporters from the Des Moines Register are here because of you. What they will ask you is this, 'Would you rather be paid outright for your overdue bills or would you rather live for a time with your debtors?' This is a most wonderful question!

"Why do I ask? Because the entrance to your embroidery shop is lined with people, forty up to the present count. You see, they heard for the past days of your kindness to our good citizen, Heer van Gorp, and how you have served him so faithfully! So, yesterday these people formed a group in my office to plan a special Aafji Christmas celebration. So! We wanted to keep this a secret until nearer *Kerstdag*, but reporters from the "Register" got hold of it and one of them and a cameraman are here now. They want your answer to their question for the morning edition.

Decision Time

"I should tell you, Aafji de Haan, that all those owing you want you to come and stay with them. From your debtors' children to the older citizens like Heer van Gorp, they want you in their homes! Yes! But on the other hand, they are all also ready to pay you immediately and in full if you do not want to stay with them.

"So! What would be your answer? Which way would you choose to go?"

It was an auspicious oration, and when it was finished Aafji was hiding her face against the wall of the porch, the broom locked in her hands, her shoulders shaking as she sobbed.

Silence, deep as the hush of a Christmas Eve, hung over the porch-lit scene and over the town itself. All that was heard was the whispered voice of Ypi van Gorp who, full of relief, murmured with a chuckle, words that might have been a prayer, "Job, Job, what is a man to say?" Best of all was for him to see Engeltji go to Aafji, put her arms around her and with her kerchief wipe the tears from Aafji's eyes.

"As to the question they want you to answer," Engeltji advised joyously, "I know what I would do. I would pick and choose. Sometimes money is better. Sometimes companionship. Not so, Ypi? And I would also give each of my debtors a star like the one that shines on your forehead from your scarf! But let them pay for it. Never have I seen a Christmas star more lovely. Not so, Mr. Mayor? Not so, Ypi?"

Heer Mayor applauded while Ypi nodded agreement, afraid to speak.

Then, amid the laughter and applause, Ypi unfastened his cravat and held it up for all to see an Aafji-star embroidered in the woolen fold.

Warmed by the new-found acceptance, Aafji removed her scarf and tied it around the forehead of Engeltji. The cameraman who had mounted the porch, shouted his

"Vroolijke Kerstmis!"

commands which ordered Engeltji and Aafji to enfold Heer Ypi van Gorp, with their arms around his shoulders, while the flashing bulbs caught him standing erect and bold as if he didn't need his crutches anymore.

And a gentle smile began to brighten Aafji's face.

Postscript

Yes, Virginia, there is an Aafji.

True, *A Gift to Aafji* is fiction.

And, yet...

Aafji (pronounced ah'-fee) did live in the person of Miss Siebertje Viersen, a generation before the 1933 Depression era in which author Marcus Bach sets his story.

Miss Viersen came to Pella when she was 17, when Pella also was young. She was an embroiderer and tailor. And she did accept payment "in kind"--in room and board, in fine colts, nice cows, and large cribs of corn. She did so well, in fact, that she amassed a fortune in her day. And with Andrew Carnegie, donated the beautiful public library to Pella.

And, of course, the Spirit of Christmas, the reaching out in helpfulness and kindness, is true. And still lives in Pella.

Especially at Christmas time.

* * *

Pella is a Dutch community located in south-central Iowa, about 40 miles southeast of Des Moines...20 miles south of Interstate 80...and 75 miles southwest of the Amana Colonies. Pella's Tulip Time celebration is every Spring, on Mothers Day weekend in May.

DR. MARCUS BACH

Marcus Bach, since childhood in Sauk City, Wisconsin, has explored -- and continues to explore -- our greatest aspirations. He is director of the Fellowship for Spiritual Understanding (Palos Verdes Estates, California).

Dr. Bach received his Ph.D. from the University of Iowa, where he was professor in the School of Religion. He holds five honorary degrees from other universities. He is the author of more than 20 books. Dr. Bach is an internationally renowned researcher in the field of inter-cultural and inter-religious relations. He is the foremost authority on contemporary religious beliefs and practices.

Dawnelle and Joseph Engesser

Dawnelle and Joseph Engesser live in Prescott, Wisconsin with their two-year-old son, Jared. Joseph graduated from Iowa Lakes Community College with a degree in Commercial Art. Joseph is a freelance artist. His work appears in numerous business newsletters, daily and weekly newspapers and magazines. Dawnelle studied art at the University of Wisconsin, River Falls. She enjoys working as a homemaker, while maintaining her interest in writing and fine art.